BASKETBALL SEASON TICKET

THE ULTIMATE FAN GUIDE

BY THOMAS NEUMANN

First Edition
First Printing, 2019

Book design by Sarah Taplin
Cover design by Sarah Taplin
Photographs ©: Tony Dejak/AP Images, cover (bottom left); Marcio Jose Sanchez/AP Images, cover (top), 33; Sue Ogrocki/AP Images, cover (bottom right bottom), 95; Eric Gay/AP Images, cover (bottom right top); janniwet/Shutterstock Images, cover (center background); AP Images, 4, 12, 22, 25, 46, 49, 56–57; Empics Sports Photo Agency/Press Association/AP Images, 7; Stephan Savoia/AP Images, 9; Frank Gunn/The Canadian Press/AP Images, 11, 79; Warren M. Winterbottom/AP Images, 15; John Rooney/AP Images, 18; Ray Stubblebine/AP Images, 21; Mark J. Terrill/AP Images, 29; Kevin Reece/Icon Sportswire/AP Images, 34; Reed Saxon/AP Images, 37, 51; John Swart/AP Images, 41; Morry Gash/AP Images, 45; Jeff Roberson/AP Images, 53; Massimiliano Ferraro/NurPhoto/Sipa USA/AP Images, 54; Peter Halpern/AP Images, 61; Lynne Sladky/AP Images, 63; Jim Mone/AP Images, 64; Michael O'Brien/AP Images, 68; Michael Caulfield/AP Images, 71; Ross D. Franklin/AP Images, 74–75; Frank Franklin II/AP Images, 76; Ann Heisenfelt/AP Images, 81; Kathy Willens/AP Images, 85; Jeff Reinking/AP Images, 86; Susan Ragan/AP Images, 89; Tony Gutierrez/AP Images, 92; Red Line Editorial, 96–97

Design Elements ©: Shutterstock Images

Press Box Books, an imprint of Press Room Editions

Library of Congress Control Number: 2018940604

ISBN:
978-1-63494-035-1 (paperback)
978-1-63494-040-5 (epub)
978-1-63494-045-0 (hosted ebook)

Distributed by North Star Editions, Inc.
2297 Waters Drive
Mendota Heights, MN 55120
www.northstareditions.com

Printed in the United States of America

TABLE OF CONTENTS

CHAPTER 1

OPENING TIP

It started with two peach baskets on December 21, 1891.

A physical education teacher named James Naismith needed a game for his students to play. So he nailed the containers to opposite ends of a balcony in a gymnasium in Springfield, Massachusetts. Naismith then assembled two teams of nine players each and instructed them to throw a soccer ball into the opposing team's basket in order to score a point.

When he blew his whistle, his students began the first game of what was then called *basket ball*.

It was a moment that would change the sports world forever, but the early results weren't pretty. As Naismith remembered it, several players received

James Naismith was just looking for a way to engage his students when he created the global phenomenon known as basketball.

black eyes, one suffered a separated shoulder, and another was knocked unconscious.

"The boys began tackling, kicking, and punching in the clinches," Naismith said years later. "They ended up in a free-for-all in the middle of the gym floor."

This wasn't at all what Naismith had in mind. He wanted to invent a game that could be played indoors during the winter and promote fitness with a low risk of injury to players. Naismith would modify the rules, most importantly by requiring ball handlers to dribble the ball, rather than allowing them to run with it.

> "The boys began tackling, kicking, and punching in the clinches. They ended up in a free-for-all in the middle of the gym floor."
>
> –James Naismith

"That stopped tackling and slugging," Naismith recalled. "We tried out the game with those rules, and we didn't have one casualty."

The first public exhibition of the sport was held in the same gym on March 11, 1892. A team of students defeated Naismith and a group of teachers by a score of 5–1. In those days, someone would have to fetch the ball out of the basket following each score–either from the balcony or with a ladder.

Men's basketball became an Olympic sport at the 1936 Games in Berlin, Germany.

In the following years, peach baskets were replaced by iron hoops and nylon nets, and participation would be limited to five players at a time for each team. The game spread relatively quickly across the United States and Canada. Before long people were playing overseas in places such as Australia, Great Britain, and Japan.

By the early 1900s, college basketball was being played from coast to coast in America. In the 1920s, professional teams in various leagues sprung up across the country. Before the end of that decade, a pair of successful African-American teams, the Harlem Globetrotters and the New York Rens, gained fame as barnstorming squads. They traveled around the country to compete wherever they could find an audience.

The sport continued to grow in popularity, leading to the formation of two professional leagues. The National Basketball League began in 1937. The Basketball Association of America started its first season in 1946. In 1949 the two leagues merged to become the National Basketball Association (NBA).

The NBA took baby steps toward success in the following decades. Legendary players such as George Mikan, Bill Russell, and Wilt Chamberlain dominated during the league's early years. In the late 1950s, the league gave birth to one of the greatest dynasties in sports history in Russell's Boston Celtics. It also survived a challenge by an upstart rival league, the American Basketball Association, in the 1970s. All the while, the league continued to grow. From 1966 to 1980, the NBA expanded from 10 to 23 teams.

Michael Jordan dominated the NBA during the 1990s, winning scoring titles and league titles with the Chicago Bulls.

But it wasn't until Larry Bird and Magic Johnson ignited a legendary rivalry in the 1980s that the NBA became a stable and profitable property. The contests between Johnson's Lakers and Bird's Celtics became the stuff of legend. Then Michael Jordan and the Chicago Bulls took the league to a whole new level in the 1990s.

Meanwhile, basketball's popularity was spreading. More and more athletes were playing the sport around the world–and they started joining the NBA in greater numbers. At the same time, women's basketball was taking off. Following new laws in the 1970s, girls had greater access to play school sports. In 1997 the Women's National Basketball Association (WNBA) launched as a new league to build on that growth. It became the first women's pro league to stick around.

A new generation of iconic players took over after 2000, including Kobe Bryant, Yao Ming, and LeBron James. The NBA continued to expand its fan base to nearly every corner of the world. Now 30 teams strong, the NBA looks to the future with hardwood heroes such as Kevin Durant, Russell Westbrook, and Stephen Curry leading the way.

Millions of people have played the game since its invention more than a century ago. Thousands have risen through the ranks of the NBA, the unquestioned top league in the world. The very best of those players are inducted as members of the Naismith Memorial Basketball Hall of Fame in Springfield, Massachusetts.

The way basketball is played has evolved in countless ways since those peach baskets were first

Exciting players such as the Toronto Raptors' DeMar DeRozan are part of the next wave of young NBA stars.

hung in 1891. But the object of the game remains the same as it did then—to get the ball down the court and put it in the basket.

CHAPTER 2

PRO BASKETBALL'S EVOLUTION

Basketball exploded in popularity after the first game was played inside that gym in Springfield, Massachusetts. Within seven years of the game's invention, the first professional league was launched.

It was called the National Basketball League (NBL), and it lasted from 1898 to 1904, with the Trenton Nationals winning the first two championships. The league's name implied a national association, but in truth, the NBL operated strictly in the northeastern United States. Unlike college basketball, which had spread across America by the early 1900s, the professional game remained mostly confined to the Northeast for the better part of two decades.

Pete Barry played for the original Boston Celtics in the early 1900s.

In those days, games were often contested in giant cages made of wire or rope. This protected fans when players spilled beyond the court and fought for possession of the ball. For that reason, players became known as cagers, a term occasionally still used today. Even though the rule that allowed teams to battle for possession of the ball out of bounds was changed in 1902, games were still being played in cages as late as the 1930s in some places.

The first pro league that operated beyond the eastern states came into being in 1925. The American Basketball League (ABL) stretched from Boston to Chicago. However, teams were constantly shuffling, popping up, and disappearing from year to year. Although the league shut down from 1931 to 1933 as a result of the Great Depression, it resumed operations and stayed in business until 1955.

A new version of the NBL emerged in 1937, and it wasn't long before it eclipsed the ABL as the top competitive circuit in the country. The NBL teams were based in the Midwest, many of them in small cities and towns such as Akron, Ohio, and Oshkosh, Wisconsin. The league expanded east, reaching as far as New York in the 1940s. However, the NBL would

Red Rocha (4) of the St. Louis Bombers looks to pass against the Philadelphia Warriors in a 1948 BAA game.

suffer the same fate as the ABL when the Basketball Association of America (BAA) came along in 1946.

The BAA set up business in larger cities and played its games in larger arenas. It aimed to become the unquestioned major professional basketball league. When the NBL fell into decline, the BAA absorbed the league after the 1948–49 season. This formed the National Basketball Association.

Eight of the teams from that first 1949–50 NBA season still exist today. Two remain in the same cities: the Boston Celtics and the New York Knicks. The other six have gone through various moves and name changes in the decades since. The Fort Wayne Pistons now play in Detroit. The Minneapolis Lakers are now in Los Angeles. The Philadelphia Warriors moved to California and are called the Golden State Warriors. The Rochester Royals had stops in Cincinnati and Kansas City before becoming the Sacramento Kings. The Syracuse Nationals are now the Philadelphia 76ers. And the Tri-Cities Blackhawks had a stint in St. Louis before landing in Atlanta, where they are now the Hawks.

In the early days of the NBA, games could be tedious affairs. Some teams would stall the action after getting out to a lead. Players passed the ball over and over with no intention of taking a shot. That left opponents with little opportunity to get back in the game. The result was a bland product that did little to inspire fans or grow the game.

That all changed in 1954, when Danny Biasone and Leo Ferris introduced a key innovation that would change the game forever: the shot clock.

Biasone owned the Syracuse Nationals, and Ferris was his general manager. Together, they devised a plan that required teams to shoot the ball within 24 seconds of gaining possession. It was a bold idea. They settled on the 24-second interval because it would guarantee at least 120 possessions per 48-minute game. That would speed up play and make the game more exciting. The idea was successfully tested in a scrimmage, and the league adopted it as a rule prior to the 1954–55 season.

> "The game had become a stalling game. A team would get ahead, even in the first half, and it would go into a stall. The other team would keep fouling, and it got to be a constant parade to the foul line. Boy, was it dull!"
>
> –Danny Biasone

"The game had become a stalling game," Biasone said years later. "A team would get ahead, even in the first half, and it would go into a stall. The other team would keep fouling, and it got to be a constant parade to the foul line. Boy, was it dull!"

The desired uptick in game pace was achieved. In 1954–55, the Celtics became the first NBA team to average 100 points per game over an entire

The Minneapolis Lakers became pro basketball's first dynasty, winning five titles in six seasons beginning in 1948–49.

season. By the 1957–58 season, each of the league's eight teams had reached that mark.

Meanwhile, interest in the sport was building, and pro basketball began growing its footprint across the country. The Minneapolis Lakers moved to Los Angeles in 1960, and the Philadelphia Warriors relocated to San Francisco two years later.

The Chicago Packers joined the league in 1961 but would move to Baltimore two years later. They do business these days as the Washington Wizards. Chicago received a new team, the Bulls, to replace the Packers in 1966. From 1967 to 1974, the NBA expanded to cities such as Cleveland, Milwaukee, Phoenix, and Portland while swelling from 10 to 18 teams.

As pro basketball's popularity grew, another league tried to get in on the action. The American Basketball Association (ABA) began play in 1967. The league offered outsized personalities, wild uniforms, and a red, white, and blue ball. The ABA permanently altered pro basketball with other innovations, too. It popularized the three-point shot, introduced the slam-dunk contest, and brought pro basketball to future NBA locales such as Dallas, Denver, Houston, Miami, New Orleans, and Utah.

The ABA never found sound financial footing, though, and the league folded in 1976. However, four of its teams were absorbed into the NBA: the Denver Nuggets, Indiana Pacers, New York Nets, and San Antonio Spurs.

With 22 teams scattered from coast to coast, the NBA was about to enter its golden era. The league adopted the ABA's three-point shot in 1979, adding another dimension of excitement to the game. And then a new generation of stars and rivalries helped the league become a fixture on network television during the 1980s.

A result of that success was the addition of five new teams in a span of nine years: the Dallas Mavericks in 1980, the Charlotte Hornets and Miami Heat in 1988, and the Orlando Magic and Minnesota Timberwolves in 1989.

The NBA expanded into Canada when the Toronto Raptors and Vancouver Grizzlies joined the league in 1995. However, the Grizzlies would relocate to Memphis in 2001. When Charlotte rejoined the league in 2004, replacing the team it had lost to New Orleans two years earlier, it brought the NBA to its current total of 30 teams.

Julius Erving of the New York Nets dunks over Denver Nuggets center Dan Issel in a 1976 ABA game.

16
19
14

CHAPTER 3

DYNASTIES RULE

In the history of the NBA, a handful of teams have stood head and shoulders above the competition. These are the dynasties of pro basketball.

The first NBA team to emerge as a power was the Minneapolis Lakers, a franchise purchased for a mere $15,000 in 1947. Beginning in 1949, when the league was still known as the BAA, the Lakers won five championships in a six-year span.

The Lakers relied heavily on George Mikan, pro basketball's first dominant big man. He led the league in scoring three times and rebounding twice during a relatively brief seven-year career. But the Lakers weren't a one-man show. Sturdy power forward Vern Mikkelsen fortified their front line. Point guard Slater Martin ran the offense. Meanwhile, small forward Jim

George Mikan (shooting) was at the center of the Minneapolis Lakers' success in the 1940s and 1950s.

Pollard, known as the Kangaroo Kid, was said to have the ability to dunk from the foul line. All four, as well as coach John Kundla, are in the Hall of Fame.

Surpassing the Lakers' dominance was a tall task. The Boston Celtics were up for it. In the early 1950s, the Celtics were a good team. Relying on the backcourt skills of Bob Cousy and Bill Sharman, they were often contenders for the Eastern Division title. But they needed someone to get them over the hump. Shrewd coach Red Auerbach found that missing piece.

Auerbach pulled off one of the league's great trades by fleecing the St. Louis Hawks of newly drafted center Bill Russell in 1956. Russell's arrival in Boston shifted the NBA's balance of power for more than a decade. Fresh off two national championships at the University of San Francisco, Russell possessed tremendous instincts and anticipation. In the NBA, he became an expert shot blocker and one of the greatest defensive players in league history. He would go on to become a five-time Most Valuable Player (MVP), and today he ranks second only to rival Wilt Chamberlain in career rebounds and rebounds per game. Russell was the only player able to effectively defend Chamberlain, who outweighed him by 60 pounds.

Center Bill Russell (left) and coach Red Auerbach (right) were key figures in the Celtics' 1960s dynasty.

Russell provided the inside presence. Cousy was a slick ball handler who knew just when and where to pass. Together they formed the backbone of the Celtics dynasty. Boston also acquired hustling forward Tommy Heinsohn, skilled swingman John Havlicek, and crafty guards Sam Jones and K.C. Jones. The latter two eventually inherited the backcourt from Cousy and Sharman.

Together, those Celtics piled up 11 NBA championships from 1957 to 1969. They were interrupted only twice, by the St. Louis Hawks in 1958 and the Philadelphia 76ers in 1967. Still, that stretch of success remains unmatched in major professional sports.

Only Russell was a member of all 11 of those early Celtics championship teams. He led his teams to an 11–0 record in winner-take-all playoff games over the course of his career. While still playing, Russell added the title of head coach in 1966, guiding the Celtics to two championships in three seasons.

The Lakers, representing Minneapolis in 1959 and Los Angeles thereafter, were on the wrong side of many of those defeats. The Celtics beat the Lakers seven times in the NBA Finals from 1959 to 1969. Those Lakers teams were blessed with two of the greatest scorers in NBA history: Elgin Baylor and Jerry West. But it wasn't until 1972, after Chamberlain joined the team, that the Lakers would win their first championship in Los Angeles. The Lakers also won a record 33 consecutive games during that 1971–72 season.

Meanwhile, the New York Knicks were busy supplanting the Celtics as the top team in the Eastern Conference. The Knicks rode the talents of silky-smooth point guard Walt Frazier and sturdy center Willis Reed. New York matched up with the Lakers three times in the NBA Finals, winning in 1970 and 1973.

The decisive Game 7 in 1970 stands as one of the great moments in NBA history. Reed missed Game 6 with a torn thigh muscle and then skipped warm-ups for Game 7. But when the game started, Reed was there. His inspired play through the pain helped push the Knicks to victory.

> "I wanted to play. That was for the championship, the one great moment you play for all your life. I didn't want to have to look at myself in the mirror 20 years later and say I wished I had tried to play."
>
> –Willis Reed

"I wanted to play," Reed said. "That was for the championship, the one great moment you play for all your life. I didn't want to have to look at myself in the mirror 20 years later and say I wished I had tried to play."

The Celtics climbed back into the championship picture in the mid-1970s. After Russell's retirement in 1969, Havlicek led the team into the next decade. With Heinsohn as coach, Havlicek helped Boston back to glory with championships in 1974 and 1976. Celtics center Dave Cowens and point guard JoJo White would eventually join Havlicek in the Hall of Fame.

The Lakers and Celtics rekindled their rivalry from the 1960s when Magic Johnson and Larry Bird entered the league in 1979, bringing unprecedented popularity to the NBA. The Lakers brought razzle-dazzle to the league, attracting movie stars to their games to watch a fast-paced brand of basketball that came to be known as Showtime. The Celtics thrived on toughness, defense, and the all-around brilliance of Bird.

In addition to Johnson and unstoppable center Kareem Abdul-Jabbar, the Lakers had talent throughout the lineup. Shooting guard Michael Cooper and power forward A.C. Green were standout defenders, while forward James Worthy was a spectacular playmaker. Known as Big Game James for his postseason exploits, Worthy often finished off fast breaks with ferocious dunks.

The Celtics were stacked with defensive wizards Dennis Johnson at guard and Robert Parish at center. Power forward Kevin McHale was a force at both ends of the floor. Boston added another game changer in center Bill Walton in 1985. Like Bird, all four would go on to become Hall of Famers.

Boston and Los Angeles clashed in three epic NBA Finals series in the 1980s.

In 1984 the Celtics muscled their way to victory in seven games, using their physical play to slow

Michael Jordan and the Chicago Bulls toyed with their opponents during their dominant 1990s period.

down the Lakers and take them out of their comfort zone. Los Angeles found a tempo more to its liking with a six-game victory in 1985. Magic Johnson stole the show in the 1987 Finals by leading the Lakers in points, rebounds, and assists as Los Angeles won in six games.

Waiting in the wings was the dynamic duo of Michael Jordan and Scottie Pippen, who would construct a 1990s basketball empire in Chicago. Horace Grant helped anchor the team with all-around play on both sides of the court. Coach Phil Jackson, meanwhile, was pulling the levers. He went on to win a record 11 championships as head coach, six of them with Chicago.

And Jordan? He was simply establishing himself as the greatest player ever.

The 1990s Bulls could play a physical game or win with finesse. They were able to wrestle their way through the punishing Eastern Conference playoffs, and then outhustle and glide past Western foes in the NBA Finals.

After winning three consecutive NBA Finals from 1991 to 1993, Jordan stepped away to play minor league baseball for the better part of two seasons. When he returned to Chicago, the retooled Bulls were better than ever. Grant was gone by then. But rebounding savant Dennis Rodman and sharpshooter Toni Kukoc more than made up for the loss.

The 1995–96 Bulls went 72–10 in the regular season and 15–3 in the playoffs on their way to the championship. They were widely regarded as the best team in NBA history. Chicago then defeated the Utah Jazz in hard-fought series in 1997 and 1998 to again win its third straight title.

Jordan retired from the Bulls again following the 1998 Finals, creating a vacancy atop the league's power structure. The Lakers and San Antonio Spurs surged in to fill the vacuum.

The Lakers began maneuvering to build yet another dynasty with the 1996 acquisitions of unmovable center Shaquille O'Neal and high school star Kobe Bryant. After a few years of growing pains, they tapped Jackson to bring his coaching wizardry to Los Angeles and lift the Lakers to a championship level.

O'Neal was in his prime, regularly ranking among the league's top scorers and rebounders, while Bryant was emerging as one of the NBA's top players in his own right. The pairing of O'Neal's brute force and Bryant's extraordinary agility was a devastating combination. When O'Neal wasn't overpowering defenders, Bryant was embarrassing them with a diverse array of moves and shots. It added up to three consecutive championships from 2000 to 2002, with the 2001 team going 15–1 in the playoffs.

> "I think our time had just run its course. But we were the most dominant one-two punch in Lakers history."
>
> —Shaquille O'Neal

"I think our time had just run its course," O'Neal

said. "But we were the most dominant one-two punch in Lakers history."

At the same time, the Spurs were building something special in San Antonio. Behind the twin towers of Tim Duncan and David Robinson, they beat Shaq and Kobe to the punch by winning the 1999 championship. They responded to the Lakers' next run by adding backcourt mates Tony Parker and Manu Ginobili and defensive stopper Bruce Bowen.

The Spurs captured the 2003 championship in Robinson's final season and returned to win it all in 2005 and again in 2007. Versatile forward Kawhi Leonard teamed with the core of Duncan, Parker, and Ginobili to lift San Antonio to its fifth NBA championship in 2014—but not before Bryant and the Lakers took care of some unfinished business.

By the late 2000s, the Lakers had renovated their roster with Bryant as the centerpiece. Agile 7-footer Pau Gasol and rangy 6'10" forward Lamar Odom were his sidekicks. The trio created all sorts of matchup problems for opponents on their way to back-to-back championships in 2009 and 2010.

On the West Coast, the Golden State Warriors were primed to start a new dynasty. With the All-Star trio of point guard Stephen Curry, guard Klay

Stephen Curry and the Warriors emerged as the NBA's new dominant team in 2015.

Thompson, and forward Draymond Green, the Warriors took the league by storm in 2014–15. Three-pointers rained down from all over the court as the Warriors went 67–15 and won the NBA title. One year later, they won 73 games. That broke the 1995–96 Bulls record. However, LeBron James and the Cleveland Cavaliers upset them in the playoffs. With that, the Warriors only got better. They added star forward Kevin Durant in the offseason and went on to win the next two NBA titles. A modern NBA dynasty had emerged.

LAKERS
CELTICS
33

CHAPTER 4

SUPERSTARS SEIZE THE DAY

The greatest individual rivalry in basketball history was born on March 26, 1979.

On that day, Earvin "Magic" Johnson and Larry Bird locked horns for the first time. Johnson's Michigan State Spartans faced Bird's Indiana State Sycamores for the college basketball national championship.

The players were the two biggest stars in college basketball. Fans around the country eagerly anticipated the showdown. It was no surprise, then, that the game drew enormous television ratings. Nearly 40 percent of televisions in use in the United States were tuned in to the game. Johnson recorded 24 points, seven

The Lakers Magic Johnson (left) and the Celtics Larry Bird (right) lifted the NBA to new heights in the 1980s.

rebounds, and five assists as the Spartans claimed a 75–64 win. Bird had 19 points and 13 rebounds.

With that, Johnson and Bird validated themselves as budding superstars. A few months later, they began to lift the professional game to new heights. Johnson joined the Lakers as the first pick in that year's draft. Bird joined the Celtics, who had picked him one year earlier and held on to his rights.

Almost from the moment Bird and Johnson entered the NBA, fan interest mushroomed and attendance steadily increased. The league became a fixture on network television, beaming its product into tens of millions of living rooms across America.

Johnson was an oversized point guard with impeccable instincts. At 6'9", he was a dazzling passer who created absurd mismatches. His size and speed made him amazingly versatile, able to play all five positions at a high level. Plus, Magic always seemed to have a smile on his face. His boundless enthusiasm lifted him to celebrity status alongside movie stars and famous entertainers in Los Angeles.

Bird was an incredibly clutch shooter and fantastic rebounder who could play either forward spot. Bird was all business, a cool and fearsome competitor who regularly wore a scowl.

Johnson and the Lakers won five NBA titles in the 1980s, including two over the Celtics.

The two players transitioned seamlessly to the pro game. Johnson teamed up with masterful big man Kareem Abdul-Jabbar to win the NBA championship as a rookie. Bird won his first title the following year against the Houston Rockets.

Bird and Johnson were perfect adversaries, and the rivalry was cemented when they met in the 1984 NBA Finals. The Celtics scratched and clawed their way past the Lakers in seven games, and Bird averaged 27 points and 14 rebounds to outshine Johnson. Magic turned the tables in the 1985 Finals. Johnson piloted the Lakers to victory over the Celtics in six games, averaging 14 assists per game in support of series MVP Abdul-Jabbar.

Johnson and Bird had known each other only as opponents to that point. But that changed when the two filmed a famous 1986 sneaker commercial in Bird's rural hometown of French Lick, Indiana. Although they would maintain a fierce rivalry between the lines, they became friends away from the game. That didn't mean they eased up on the court, though.

> "We came along at the right time. That's all I can say. I needed Larry and he needed me. We pushed each other, meant so much to each other and meant so much to the game."
>
> —Magic Johnson

Johnson saved his best performance in the rivalry for the 1987 NBA Finals. He averaged 26 points, 8 rebounds, and 13 assists, leading the Lakers in all three categories, as Los Angeles won in six games.

"We came along at the right time," Johnson once said. "That's all I can say. I needed Larry and he needed me. We pushed each other, meant so much to each other and meant so much to the game."

As Johnson and Bird eased toward retirement in the late 1980s, the NBA spotlight switched its focus to Chicago. An exciting young shooting guard named Michael Jordan was already making history with the Bulls.

Jordan immediately captivated fans with his singular athleticism and tongue-wagging exploits. He boasted seemingly endless hang time while throwing down a dazzling array of dunks. Jordan emerged on the national stage with a 63-point effort in one game against Bird and the Celtics in the 1986 playoffs. He would go on to win 10 NBA scoring titles, including seven in a row from 1986–87 to 1992–93, and he remains the NBA career leader in scoring average at 30.1 points per game.

Jordan went on to become basketball's first global superstar. Companies of all types wanted him to pitch their products, with Jordan selling everything from fast food to sports drinks to underwear. He might be best known for his signature line of sneakers, though. They remain popular even today.

But Jordan would soon prove to be much more than a flashy showman and brilliant scorer. In his pursuit of excellence, he also became one of the NBA's best defenders and arguably its greatest leader. In the 1990s, Jordan's Bulls took over the league, popularizing the term *three-peat* by twice winning three consecutive league titles. Had Jordan not left the NBA to play minor league baseball for the better part of two seasons, the Bulls just might have won eight championships in a row.

His work ethic and determination were legendary. Just ask the Utah Jazz, who witnessed that firsthand in Game 5 of the 1997 NBA Finals. Stricken by the flu, wobbly and dehydrated, Jordan still managed to score 38 points and lead the Bulls to victory. No other player scored even half that many points in the game.

Jordan's five NBA MVP Awards rank second in league history to Abdul-Jabbar. Jordan was also named Finals MVP in each of his six appearances.

Just as Jordan's career was winding down, another phenomenal talent was jumping directly from high school to the pros. In the coming years, Kobe Bryant would draw countless comparisons to Jordan as he emerged as star guard for the Lakers. Like Jordan, he was a gifted scorer and fearless competitor who also

Michael Jordan's electrifying skills helped propel the Chicago Bulls to the top of the NBA.

learned to become a top defender. Both players were fiery, determined competitors who could create their own shot from anywhere on the floor.

While Jordan was the better scorer in his prime, Bryant excelled over a longer period. Bryant was an 18-time All-Star and retired third on the NBA career scoring list with 33,643 points.

Bryant won five NBA championships with the Lakers, three of them while playing alongside dominant center Shaquille O'Neal. The prime of his career coincided with the explosion of basketball popularity in China. Bryant visited that country more than 10 times over the years on promotional tours, drawing crowds of thousands of fans hoping to get a glimpse of the Lakers star.

Bryant produced one of the NBA's greatest performances when he scored 81 points in a 2006 game against the Toronto Raptors. That ranked second in NBA history behind only Wilt Chamberlain's 100-point effort in 1962. In his last game before retiring in 2016, Bryant memorably scored 60 points in a win over the Utah Jazz.

"When you think about this town for the last 20 years, this man [Bryant] has been the biggest and greatest celebrity we've had," Magic Johnson said. "He's the greatest to wear the purple and gold."

> "When you think about this town for the last 20 years, this man [Bryant] has been the biggest and greatest celebrity we've had....He's the greatest to wear the purple and gold."
>
> –Magic Johnson

While Bryant was ascending in Los Angeles, another high schooler was making the jump to the NBA with the Cleveland Cavaliers.

LeBron James was already a star even before he reached the NBA, with national television broadcasting many of his prep games from Akron, Ohio. The 6'8" James boasted a versatile skill set that was reminiscent of Johnson's, and he signed a lucrative shoe deal before he ever set foot on an NBA court.

Even as a 19-year-old rookie in the 2003–04 season, James seemed to score effortlessly, topping 20 points per game against far more experienced opponents. He led the Cavaliers to the NBA Finals at age 22 in 2007. After leaving to join Dwyane Wade and the Miami Heat, James broke through to win two NBA championships. Then he returned to Cleveland in

2014. Back with his hometown team, James powered the Cavs to their first NBA title in 2016.

In 2018 he became the youngest player, at age 33, to reach 30,000 career points.

Each generation in the NBA seems to have an iconic superstar or two. But behind those superstars are many other amazing players. James gets a lot of attention today. But there is no shortage of outstanding players.

Stephen Curry and Kevin Durant have led the Golden State Warriors to uncharted territory. Russell Westbrook of the Oklahoma City Thunder dazzles fans with his grace and prowess as a scorer, passer, and rebounder. Big men Giannis Antetokounmpo, Anthony Davis, and Karl-Anthony Towns are becoming unstoppable forces with the Milwaukee Bucks, New Orleans Pelicans, and Minnesota Timberwolves, respectively. And in Texas, James Harden and his famous beard are wildly popular with the Houston Rockets.

Looking to the future, the NBA is clearly in good hands when it comes to entertaining the masses.

Houston Rockets guard James Harden (left) and Milwaukee Bucks forward Giannis Antetokounmpo are stars of today's NBA.

LAKERS
99
PACKERS
7

CHAPTER 5

BIG MEN IN THE MIDDLE

Believe it or not, basketball was once thought to be better suited to small, quick players than to their taller counterparts.

George Mikan, a 6'10" behemoth with surprising agility and a deadly hook shot, changed that line of thinking.

Mikan was the first basketball superstar, and his popularity with the Minneapolis Lakers was such that the marquee at Madison Square Garden read, "Geo. Mikan v/s Knicks" prior to a 1949 game in New York. Although not exceptionally big by today's NBA standards, he was so unstoppable against the

Defending against Minneapolis Lakers center George Mikan was a losing battle for most opponents.

players of his era that rules were changed to minimize his dominance.

Known as Mr. Basketball, Mikan was nearly impossible to defend close to the basket. That led the NBA to widen the free-throw lane from 6 to 12 feet, which forced big men to play farther away from the hoop. He was also a key figure in the implementation of the 24-second shot clock. Opponents often stalled the action to keep the ball away from him.

Mikan led the Lakers to five league championships. When the Basketball Hall of Fame opened in 1959, he was a member of its inaugural class of inductees.

As Mikan had demonstrated, a talented big man could dominate an NBA game. Wilt Chamberlain confirmed that trend. And he did so with a much different style than Mikan's.

Chamberlain played a year with the famed Harlem Globetrotters before entering the NBA in 1959 with his hometown Philadelphia Warriors. At 7'1" and 275 pounds, Chamberlain was supremely athletic, skilled, and strong. He led the league in scoring each of his first seven seasons and in rebounding 11 times in 14 seasons. His superiority led the league to widen the free-throw lane again, this time to 16 feet.

Wilt Chamberlain rises for an easy bucket during a 1960 game with the Philadelphia Warriors.

Chamberlain famously scored 100 points in a single game on March 2, 1962. His Warriors beat the Knicks 169–147 in Hershey, Pennsylvania. That season, he averaged 50.4 points per game, and both marks remain NBA records by a wide margin to this day.

Unfortunately for Chamberlain, his career coincided with that of Bill Russell and the Boston Celtics dynasty. Chamberlain produced better individual statistics, but Russell played on more complete teams with superior teammates. The Celtics knocked Chamberlain's teams out of the playoffs five times before his 76ers eliminated Boston on their way to the 1967 NBA title. He would win another championship with the Los Angeles Lakers in 1972.

Through the 2016–17 season, there had been 65 games in which a single player scored 60 or more points—and Chamberlain accounted for 32 of them. He still held league records for career rebounds (23,924) and rebounds per game (22.9). Amazingly, Chamberlain never fouled out of a game in a career that spanned 14 seasons and 1,045 contests.

At 7'2" and 225 pounds, Kareem Abdul-Jabbar wasn't as muscular as Chamberlain. But he ultimately became the most prolific scorer in NBA history. Abdul-Jabbar, the No. 1 pick in the 1969 draft, adopted

Kareem Abdul-Jabbar scored many of his points using his signature skyhook shot.

Mikan's hook shot and perfected it. In just his second pro season, he won the NBA championship with the Milwaukee Bucks and was named the league's MVP.

After six seasons in Milwaukee, Abdul-Jabbar was traded to the Lakers, where he teamed with Magic Johnson to win five NBA titles in nine seasons. Abdul-Jabbar was named an All-Star a record 19 times in his 20-year career. He also became the only player to win the NBA MVP Award six times. At the end of the 2017–18 season, he still ranked fourth in league history in career rebounds, third in blocked shots, and first in minutes played.

But scoring is what ultimately wins games, and no one did it as consistently or over a longer period than Abdul-Jabbar. He holds NBA career records with 38,387 points and 15,837 field goals.

Abdul-Jabbar retired in 1989. Soon after, one of the biggest personalities in sports history took over as the league's next dominant big man. And boy, was Shaquille O'Neal big.

At 7'1" and well over 300 pounds, O'Neal was phenomenally strong. In his prime, he was virtually unstoppable. Opponents would double- and triple-team O'Neal and regularly foul him on purpose. Sometimes the only way to stop O'Neal was to send him to the free-throw line, which was his one weakness. O'Neal could easily take over a game with thunderous dunks and easy baskets. He led the league in shooting percentage 10 times.

O'Neal was also an outgoing, media-savvy superstar who used his athletic career to open doors in the music and movie industries. He was even the

An unmovable force, Shaquille O'Neal set a new standard for dominant big men during the 1990s and early 2000s.

star of his own martial arts–themed video game early in his career. But when he wasn't entertaining fans off the court, he was dominating opponents on it.

Shaq won four NBA titles, including three in a row with the Lakers and one with the Miami Heat. Over 19 pro seasons, he made 15 All-Star Game appearances.

With only five players on the court at a time in basketball, one player can make all the difference. As Mikan showed and many others have confirmed, there's nothing quite like a dominant big man.

07 53
HARLEM
GLOBETROTTERS
24
GLOBETROTTERS
MYGLASS
MYGLASS
CENTRI CRISTALLI AUTO
LBA
LEGABASKET
SERIE A
Poste
mobile

CHAPTER 6

BASKETBALL'S SHOWMEN

Basketball combines athleticism and improvisation to create a unique, beautiful game. It's a game in which players must rely heavily on teamwork to succeed, but it also leaves plenty of room for individual artistry and expression. Whether it's passing, dribbling, shooting, or dunking, some players simply stand out.

When thinking of entertaining basketball, many think of the Harlem Globetrotters. Today the Globetrotters are the worldwide ambassadors of basketball, delighting fans far and wide with their circus skills and astonishing trick plays. The Globetrotters have been entertaining fans since even before the NBA began play.

The Harlem Globetrotters have been entertaining fans with their unique brand of basketball for many decades.

Bob Cousy (right) plays basketball with kids at a New Hampshire summer camp in 1959.

Since its founding in 1926, the team has performed in 120-plus countries and defeated the rival Washington Generals more than 14,000 times. Eleven former Globetrotters players are members of the Basketball Hall of Fame, including Lynette Woodard, the first female Globetrotter. The team itself was inducted in 2002.

Although perhaps not quite as zany as the Globetrotters, many NBA players have dazzled fans with their skills over the years.

Guards tend to be the smallest players on the court, and point guards typically control the ball more than any other player. Point guards bring the ball up the court and set up the play. Some do their job with more flair than others.

Bob Cousy was the NBA's first great ball-handling wizard. Decades ahead of his time, Cousy brought the perfect mix of showmanship and instinct to the early Boston Celtics championship teams. He played in 13 consecutive All-Star Games and is the only guard to have been named All-NBA first team in 10 consecutive seasons. He also led the league in assists eight years in a row, beginning in 1952–53. All the while, he averaged 18.4 points per game.

As Cousy's career was winding down, two of the greatest scorers ever were emerging with the Los Angeles Lakers. Elgin Baylor was Mr. Inside, a high-flying forward who attacked the rim like few before him. Jerry West was Mr. Outside, a deadly shooter with a flair for dramatic buzzer-beaters. In their 12 seasons as teammates, they entertained fans as the greatest scoring tandem in NBA history.

While Baylor and West were lighting up the scoreboard in Los Angeles, Cincinnati Royals point guard Oscar Robertson was fast emerging as a new kind of star. Robertson could do it all. He could score, averaging more than 30 points per game six times. He could pass, leading the league in assists per game seven times. And he could also rebound. In 1961–62, Robertson famously became the first player to average a triple-double over the course of an entire season. When he was on the court, fans couldn't look away or they might miss something special.

The same could be said about Pete Maravich during the 1970s. One of the game's greatest entertainers, Maravich boasted a wide array of moves, tricks, and skills. He was always capable of delivering no-look passes right on the money and was never afraid to attempt long outside shots—even before the NBA adopted the 3-point line.

"When Pete played in college, they didn't have the three-pointer and he averaged almost 45 a game," his former coach Tom Nissalke said, "and if they would've had the three-point line, then he probably would've averaged 55 or 60."

> "When Pete played in college, they didn't have the three-pointer and he averaged almost 45 a game, and if they would've had the three-point line, then he probably would've averaged 55 or 60."
>
> —Tom Nissalke

When it came to style, though, the ABA changed the game.

With former Minneapolis Lakers legend George Mikan as its first commissioner, the ABA began play in 1967 as a rival league to the NBA. It never achieved lasting financial success, but it did transform pro basketball from a simple athletic competition into a full-scale entertainment event. The ABA embraced big hair, loud uniforms, electric personalities, and thunderous dunks with a red, white, and blue basketball.

Julius Erving and George Gervin are two of the enduring figures who rose to superstardom on the ABA stage.

Erving, nicknamed "Dr. J," was a soaring, slashing virtuoso who also played extraordinary defense. He won the first professional dunk contest at the 1976 ABA All-Star Game and was an All-Star in each of his 16 pro seasons—five ABA and 11 NBA.

Gervin, nicknamed "the Iceman" for his cool demeanor, was just as exciting to watch but played with uncommon finesse. He perfected the finger roll, a silky-smooth move in which he scored by flipping the ball underhanded, often over the head of a helpless defender.

The ABA dissolved after the 1975–76 season, with four of its teams jumping to the NBA the following season. But the league had left its mark with its innovations and flashy play.

Spurs guard George Gervin used his patented finger roll to seemingly score at will.

The dunk contest has only grown more popular. And few dunkers could compare with Dominique Wilkins. The longtime Atlanta Hawks forward's dunks were so outrageous, especially his signature windmill jam, that he earned the nickname "the Human Highlight Film."

As exciting as his in-game dunks were, he might be best remembered for his dunk contest battles with

Michael Jordan. Wilkins beat Jordan to win his first dunk contest in 1985. Three years later, Jordan won in a rematch. While Wilkins was known for throwing down thunderous dunks, Jordan starred with high-flying takeoffs. Both won two dunk contests, although they probably could have won more if they had continued participating later in their careers. Future players such as Vince Carter would continue to take dunking to the extreme. But few who watched will ever forget the jams thrown down by Wilkins and Jordan.

Three-point shooting also developed into an exciting part of NBA games.

Reggie Miller wasn't necessarily flashy. But the Indiana Pacers shooting guard knew how to take over a game—especially against the rival New York Knicks. He once scored eight points in nine seconds to lift Indiana to a stunning comeback win at New York in a 1995 playoff game.

Ray Allen, another sharpshooter, nailed a game-tying three-pointer in the 2013 NBA Finals. The basket forced overtime in Game 6, which his Miami Heat won to stay alive against the Spurs. Then Miami finished the job by winning Game 7.

But no discussion of three-point shooters is complete without the dynamic "Splash Brothers."

Ray Allen hits his game-tying three-pointer in Game 6 of the 2013 NBA Finals.

Golden State Warriors teammates Stephen Curry and Klay Thompson perfected the art of taking over a game from downtown. Going into the 2018–19 season, Curry, a 6'3" point guard, held four of the top five spots for single-season three-pointers made. Thompson had the other one. Sometimes shooting from well beyond the three-point line, the Warriors could quickly overwhelm opponents. And not only did they win; they also continued the tradition of showmanship in the NBA.

CITY CENTER
MAYO CLINIC
23

CHAPTER 7

WOMEN BALLERS MAKE A NAME

Women began playing basketball in the earliest days of the sport. Yet it wasn't until the 1970s that they began to receive some of the opportunities to compete that men had long enjoyed. In fact, much of that growth can be traced right back to 1972. That's when the US government passed Title IX, a law that required schools to offer equal opportunities for girls and boys. Suddenly, girls' sports teams were representing schools just as boys' teams long had.

The journey to establish women's basketball beyond the school level was much slower, however. Developments on lower levels helped the sport finally catch on at the pro level.

Title IX opened the door for female athletes such as Maya Moore of the Minnesota Lynx.

Title IX opened up opportunities for girls in schools and colleges in 1972. That same year, the first women's college basketball national tournament was held. By 1976, women's basketball was an Olympic sport. The United States won the silver medal that year with four players who are now enshrined in the Basketball Hall of Fame.

Pat Head was the oldest player on that US team. At 24, she was already head coach at the University of Tennessee. She would take the name Pat Summitt in marriage a few years later. Over nearly four decades, Summitt led the Lady Volunteers to 1,098 wins and eight national championships. She retired in 2012 as the winningest coach in college basketball history.

> "Icons are rare breeds, and Pat Summitt was a very rare breed."
>
> –Tennessee athletic director Dave Hart

"Icons are rare breeds," Tennessee athletic director Dave Hart said, "and Pat Summitt was a very rare breed."

Lusia Harris, 21 at the time, was the top scorer and rebounder for the Americans. After lifting Delta State University to three consecutive national championships in the 1970s, she made NBA history. The New Orleans Jazz made her a seventh-round pick in 1977. To this day, she remains the only woman ever drafted by an NBA team.

Also 21, Ann Meyers led the US team in assists. She went on to earn All-America honors four times and win a national championship at UCLA. When the first women's pro league was launched in 1978, she was the No. 1 draft pick.

Meyers then led the Houston Angels, a team that boasted male cheerleaders, to the first Women's Professional Basketball League (WBL) championship. A few months later, in September 1979, she signed a $50,000 contract with the Indiana Pacers and became the first woman to try out for an NBA team. Although she didn't make the Pacers roster, she returned to the WBL and shared the MVP Award the following season.

Nancy Lieberman had just turned 18 prior to the 1976 Olympics and played limited minutes in a reserve role for the US team. But after that, she won two national championships at Old Dominion University and began one of the most remarkable careers in sports history by earning MVP honors in the final WBL season.

Lieberman competed in several women's

Nancy Lieberman (right) thrived in an era when women's sports were just establishing themselves on the college and pro levels.

professional leagues over the years. She also became the first woman to play in a men's pro league with the Springfield Fame of the United States Basketball League in 1986. The following year, she signed with the Washington Generals, longtime foils of the famed Harlem Globetrotters.

Women's basketball had no shortage of star players.

Between Team USA and schools such as Tennessee, the sport had successful teams, too. But despite this, professional women's basketball leagues struggled to generate investment or interest. Leagues such as the Women's Basketball Association and the American Basketball League came and went. None were able to find the right recipe for business success.

That all changed in 1997 when the NBA launched the WNBA. By then, generations of girls had grown up playing sports thanks to Title IX. Women's soccer and softball became Olympic sports in 1996, when the Games were held in Atlanta. Team USA won both gold medals, as well as the women's basketball gold medal. The WNBA was ready to build on that momentum.

Guard Cynthia Cooper had won a gold medal with the US team at the 1988 Olympics. Over the next several years, she established herself playing overseas. By the time the WNBA formed, Cooper was 34 years old. But when she signed with the Houston Comets, she was ready to dominate the new league.

Cooper teamed up with wing Sheryl Swoopes, who was 12 years younger and coming off an Olympic gold medal with Team USA. Together they helped the Comets win the first four WNBA championships.

Cooper led the league in scoring three times and won the MVP Award twice.

Center Lisa Leslie had also starred on the 1996 Olympic team. Leslie, who once scored 101 points *in the first half* of a high school game, went on to win two WNBA championships with the Los Angeles Sparks. She also became the first woman to dunk in a professional game. She accomplished that feat in 2002. Leslie and Swoopes each won the WNBA MVP Award three times.

Lieberman played for the Phoenix Mercury that first season, which tipped off 10 days before she turned 39. She went on to coach in the WNBA for three seasons with the Detroit Shock and even returned to play in a game for the Shock at age 50 in 2008.

With a women's pro league finally established, a new generation took over in the 2010s. The Sparks picked forward Candace Parker first overall in 2008. By 2016 she had won two MVP Awards and led the Sparks to a championship. Phoenix Mercury guard Diana Taurasi and Seattle Storm point guard Sue Bird were other big stars.

However, no team could compare with the Minnesota Lynx. Behind point guard Lindsay Whalen

The Houston Comets' Cynthia Cooper drives to the basket during a 1997 game against the Los Angeles Sparks.

and forwards Seimone Augustus and Maya Moore, the Lynx won four championships between 2011 and 2017. They finished second twice more. Center Sylvia Fowles, a dominant defensive stopper, joined the team for the 2015 title and led the Lynx to their fourth title in 2017.

"I know that [the players] wanted to take their place next to the Houston Comets," Lynx coach Cheryl Reeve said after the fourth championship. "And they did it. It's a little surreal right now."

> "I know that [the players] wanted to take their place next to the Houston Comets, and they did it. It's a little surreal right now."
>
> –Lynx coach Cheryl Reeve

The league had come a long way by then. But in some ways, the league still had a lot of room to grow.

The WNBA rolled out eight teams in its first season and peaked at 16 squads in the early 2000s. After the comings and goings of several teams later in that decade, the league stabilized at 12 teams in 2010. More than two decades after its inception, the WNBA is still going strong, and three teams have been a part of it since the beginning: the Sparks, Mercury, and New York Liberty.

WNBA players don't make nearly as much money as their NBA counterparts. But because the league maintains a summer schedule, many players also play overseas during the winter and spring. They can often make greater salaries playing in leagues around the world. WNBA career points leader Diana Taurasi, rebounds leader Tamika Catchings, and assists leader Sue Bird are among the notable players who also have forged successful careers abroad.

Like the quartet from that first US Olympic women's team, Cooper, Leslie, and Swoopes also are members of the Hall of Fame. It inducted women for the first time in 1985. Fourteen years after that, a museum was established specifically to celebrate the women's game. The Women's Basketball Hall of Fame is located in Knoxville, Tennessee. It is just a couple of miles from the University of Tennessee, where Summitt famously coached the Lady Volunteers to national prominence. More than 150 players, coaches, and contributors have been enshrined at the Hall of Fame since it opened in 1999.

In recent years, women have made their mark on the men's game as well.

Lieberman became the first woman to serve as head coach of a men's pro team in 2010. She took the

Phoenix Mercury forward Diana Taurasi became the WNBA's all-time leading scorer in 2017.

reins of the Texas Legends, the minor league affiliate of the NBA's Dallas Mavericks. Becky Hammon, a 16-year WNBA veteran, became the first female coach in NBA history when she joined the San Antonio Spurs as an

assistant in 2014. She was followed a year later by Lieberman, of course, who joined the Sacramento Kings coaching staff in 2015.

SIXERS

CHAPTER 8

IT ALL STARTS WITH THE DRAFT

The NBA is an exclusive club. There are only 450 roster spots in the league. Most of the players looking to join that club must do so through the draft, which is held each year in late June.

What was once a relatively informal affair attended strictly by league insiders has become an impressive spectacle. Today's draft is a parade of the most talented American college players and international prospects, with thousands of fans in attendance.

It's a significant moment for the participants, representing the culmination of a longtime dream to compete in the top league in the world. It's also

Expectations were high when the Philadelphia 76ers picked Ben Simmons first overall in the 2016 NBA Draft.

a fashion show of sorts, as draftees try to upstage one another with stylish suits. The evening can be emotional and nerve-racking for the athletes. They are anxious to know where they will be playing for the next several years—or if they will be selected at all.

Undrafted players still have a chance to play in the NBA, but the odds are against them. Aside from a handful of retiring veterans, most players from the previous season don't intend to give up their jobs. When 60 newly drafted players are added to the mix each year, there is already stiff competition for those 450 spots. Often, undrafted players decide to compete overseas and in American summer leagues in hopes of impressing NBA scouts.

The draft is a pretty simple concept.

All 30 NBA teams start with one selection in each of two rounds. The draft order is based on how each team finished the previous season. So the NBA champion picks last in each round. Determining the order of the first 14 picks, however, is a little more interesting.

Each of the 14 teams that miss the playoffs enter the draft lottery to determine the order of the first three picks. The team with the worst record has the best chance of getting the top pick, but often another

Drafting LeBron James first overall in 2003 helped change the Cleveland Cavaliers' fortunes.

team jumps to the top. To make things even more interesting, teams can trade draft picks.

On draft day, each team has five minutes to pick a player. It's sort of like choosing up sides on the playground—but with millions of dollars at stake. After the first 30 selections are complete, the process moves to the second round, where teams are allowed just two minutes to make each pick.

Teams must carefully consider their options prior to making their selections. A shrewd pick can position a team for a future championship.

Take the 1984 draft, for example. The Houston Rockets and Portland Trail Blazers had the top two picks. Houston picked center Hakeem Olajuwon. Portland picked center Sam Bowie. The Rockets' selection paid off. Olajuwon went on to a Hall of Fame career, leading the team to two NBA titles. The Blazers, on the other hand, were left kicking themselves.

With the third pick in that draft, the Chicago Bulls picked Michael Jordan. Bowie went on to have an injury-plagued 10-year career. But Jordan became the most dominant player of his generation. When he left the Bulls for good in 1998, he had led the league in scoring 10 times and the Bulls had won six championships.

In 1995 the Minnesota Timberwolves took a risk that paid off. With the fifth overall pick, they selected high school forward Kevin Garnett. No player had gone directly from high school to the NBA in two decades. NBA executives watched the experiment with curiosity. Would Garnett live up to his potential, or would the NBA eat the teenager alive?

In this instance, the move worked. At 6'11", Garnett combined a soft shooting touch with tricky low-post moves. Few were as ferocious on defense. These skills

Kevin Garnett started a trend of high school stars going straight to the NBA.

helped Garnett become a perennial All-Star and the 2004 NBA MVP. Later, while with the Boston Celtics, he won an NBA title. Few players in history have matched his longevity or impact.

One year after Garnett was drafted, the Lakers took a chance on another high school star. They traded to acquire Kobe Bryant, who had been selected 13th by the Charlotte Hornets. Bryant was the first guard to make the high-school-to-pro transition. And he made it well, winning five NBA titles. He retired in 2016 as the No. 3 scorer in league history.

Garnett and Bryant opened the door for many

more high school players to make the leap to the NBA. But the results weren't always as positive. In 2001, Kwame Brown became the first high school player taken first overall. Brown ended up playing 12 NBA seasons. However, he averaged just 6.6 points per game over his career.

Darko Miličić was still a teenager when he entered the 2004 draft. However, he had played in his native Serbia rather than for an American high school. Just as with Garnett and others, teams saw great potential in Miličić. They believed that with proper coaching, he could become a star. That's why the Detroit Pistons selected him second overall.

It turned out to be a disaster. Miličić struggled to fit in after joining the NBA. He started just three games in Detroit before bouncing around in supporting roles with other teams. Meanwhile, the three players picked immediately after him—Carmelo Anthony, Chris Bosh, and Dwyane Wade—each went on to make at least 10 All-Star Games apiece.

"After I drafted Darko, from that point on, the amount of background we do on every single player that you see us draft is ridiculous," Pistons President Joe Dumars said. "We do as much or more background than any other team in the NBA because of that."

In the early days of the NBA, teams could sometimes get a star player through territorial rights. That allowed an NBA team to keep hometown and local college stars away from rivals. This also helped develop local fan interest, officials believed. Wilt Chamberlain, Tom Heinsohn, and Oscar Robertson were three Hall of Famers who were acquired as territorial picks.

> "After I drafted Darko, from that point on, the amount of background we do on every single player that you see us draft is ridiculous. We do as much or more background than any other team in the NBA because of that."
>
> –Pistons President Joe Dumars

In 1966 the league did away with territorial rights. It also began awarding the No. 1 overall selection based on a coin flip between last-place teams in each division. That system lasted until 1985. However, in some ways this system rewarded bad teams. Sometimes teams would "tank," or intentionally play poorly in order to finish last and try to get the top draft pick. So in 1985, the league introduced the lottery. Now every team that misses the playoffs has a shot at the first pick. Since 1990, the lottery has been weighted so the teams with worse records have better odds of winning the top pick.

The selection order is just one of many ways the draft has evolved through the years. For decades, the draft was held behind closed doors in New York City. It became open to the public in 1978 and was first televised in 1980. In 1992 the league began staging the event at arenas around the league to accommodate larger crowds. It returned to New York in 2001 and has been held there each year since.

The draft is also much shorter today than in years past. At first, teams were permitted to keep selecting players until they simply ran out of prospects. The record number of rounds is 21, which occurred in both 1960 and 1968. The highest number of selections in a single draft was 239 in 1970. By 1974 the league settled on a standard length of 10 rounds. That was the norm until 1985, when the process was shortened to seven rounds.

Teams sometimes used their lower picks to take a chance on multisport athletes or intriguing prospects. Football stars Jim Brown and Bubba Smith, baseball standouts Dave Winfield and Tony Gwynn,

The NBA Draft has become a major event with a huge live audience and national television broadcast.

and Olympic track-and-field athletes Bob Beamon and Carl Lewis are a few of the draftees who fall into this category.

None of those athletes ever played in an NBA game, however, and selections like those are a thing of the past. The picks are simply too valuable now, because the 1988 draft was reduced to three rounds, and the current two-round format was adopted a year after that.

HOUSTON
34

CHAPTER 9

FROM THE DREAM TEAM TO A GLOBAL GAME

Since the 1980s, no American sports league has made greater strides in growing its sport around the world than the NBA.

It started modestly, when the Washington Bullets traveled to Israel for an exhibition game in 1978. They followed that with games in China and the Philippines in 1979. In the years that followed, two international talents were selected first overall in the NBA Draft on their way to superstardom. The Houston Rockets selected Nigeria native Hakeem Olajuwon, a center,

Born in Nigeria, Hakeem Olajuwon took the NBA by storm as a star center for the Houston Rockets.

in 1984. Then the New York Knicks took Jamaica-born center Patrick Ewing a year later.

In the 1980s, NBA teams began playing exhibition games in Europe. The league sent squads to Italy, Germany, Switzerland, and the Soviet Union. In the following decade, the league made regular-season debuts in Japan (1990), England (1993), and Mexico (1997).

The tipping point for basketball's global popularity, though, came at the 1992 Summer Olympics in Barcelona, Spain. It was the first time NBA players were allowed to play in the Olympics. Team USA assembled the greatest collection of basketball talent ever, a group that quickly became known as the Dream Team.

The Americans rolled out a roster with 11 future Hall of Famers, headlined by Michael Jordan, Larry Bird, and Magic Johnson. The US players were treated like rock stars, with fans and even opponents swarming them for autographs and photos.

It was easy to understand why opponents sometimes lost focus. The games were not often close. The Americans steamrolled their way to the gold medal with an 8–0 record. They won by an

Magic Johnson was one of 11 future Hall of Famers who suited up for Team USA at the 1992 Olympics.

average of 44 points per game. That dominance only added to the team's mystique.

The Dream Team's exploits created a surge of basketball interest and inspired millions of youths around the world to pick up the sport, planting the seeds for future generations of international talent.

Two years later, Olajuwon and Ewing met in a memorable championship series, with the Rockets edging the Knicks in seven games. Olajuwon was named NBA Finals MVP, becoming the first international player to earn the honor.

More international players soon followed them to NBA success.

Like Olajuwon, Dikembe Mutombo's roots were in Africa. The 7'2" center grew up in the Democratic Republic of Congo and became an imposing defender and rebounder. Whenever he'd block a shot, Mutombo would wag his finger at the shooter. Fans loved his antics. And he was pretty good, too, playing in eight All-Star Games during his 18 NBA seasons.

Eastern Europe emerged as a hotbed for international talent, too.

Vlade Divac made his NBA debut in 1989. The crafty big man from Serbia played 16 seasons with the Los Angeles Lakers, Charlotte Hornets, and Sacramento Kings. In 2015 he became general manager of the Kings.

Drazen Petrović also debuted in 1989. The Croatian star became one of the greatest pure shooters in the history of the game. He topped 20 points per game in his final two seasons as an NBA starter for the New Jersey Nets. Tragically, he was killed in an auto accident in 1993 at age 28. Nine years later, he was inducted into the Hall of Fame.

"I think the outcome of Nets history would be different if Drazen had lived," Willis Reed, the Nets general manager, said. "No doubt about that, because he's that kind of player."

> "I think the outcome of Nets history would be different if Drazen had lived. No doubt about that, because he's that kind of player."
>
> –Willis Reed, Nets general manager

Meanwhile, Detlef Schrempf arrived from Germany in 1985. The 6'9" forward was a consistent scorer and rebounder. He played 16 NBA seasons. However, another player born in Germany surpassed Schrempf's success.

The Mavericks drafted lanky forward Dirk Nowitzki in 1998. Fans weren't sure what to expect from the 7-footer. Once he found his way, though, Nowitzki set off on an iconic career. A 13-time All-Star, Nowitzki showed big men could shoot from outside, too.

His range was seemingly limitless. Nowitzki made nearly 2,000 successful three-point shots during his career. In 2017 he became the first foreign-born player,

Dirk Nowitzki (right) showed that big men could also be great shooters.

and just the sixth player overall, to score 31,000 points. He might be best remembered, though, for leading the Mavs to their first NBA title in 2011.

After Nowitzki's success, European players began to pour into the NBA. Brothers Pau and Marc Gasol, 7-footers from Spain, both became All-Stars. French point guard Tony Parker ran the show for the great

San Antonio Spurs teams of the 2000s. At his side was Argentina-born Manu Ginobili. Together they helped the Spurs win four NBA titles.

Canada has also emerged as a basketball power. Though born in South Africa, point guard Steve Nash grew up in British Columbia. Known for his shooting touch and deft passing, Nash went on to win NBA MVP Awards in 2005 and 2006. Two more Canadians later became first overall picks. Anthony Bennett went first in 2013, while Andrew Wiggins was first in 2014.

Wiggins was hardly the first international player taken first, though. After Olajuwon opened that door in 1984, players from multiple countries have been taken first overall. Among them were Andrew Bogut (Australia, 2005), Andrea Bargnani (Italy, 2006), and Ben Simmons (Australia, 2016).

Yao Ming, a center from China, also went first overall. Like that of the Dream Team a decade earlier, his influence was huge.

Yao's arrival in the NBA in 2002 sparked an explosion in basketball popularity in the world's most populous nation. A 7'6" center, Yao was an excellent defender, scorer, and rebounder for the Houston

Rockets. Chinese fans tuned in at record numbers to watch him.

In 2004 the NBA began playing preseason games in China. In 2017–18 the league played its 24th preseason game there—and each one had been a sellout. Meanwhile, more than 190 million Chinese fans watched the 2017 NBA Finals on their mobile devices.

Yao's arrival played a big role in that growth. In 2016 he was inducted into the Basketball Hall of Fame. The Rockets retired his No. 11 jersey the following year.

Overseas growth has helped the NBA become a truly international league. The league opened the 2017–18 season with 108 international players representing 42 countries and territories. And the NBA continues to aggressively promote the game and search for talent overseas.

In 2016 the league launched three training facilities in China. The goal was to provide top coaching to elite prospects there. The NBA opened a similar facility the next year in India. So, while it's still more likely that the next great NBA superstar will come from Sacramento or New York than Shanghai or New Delhi, the opportunities for international players to thrill fans and make their mark in America have never been better.

NBA fans hope Yao Ming was just the first of many Chinese superstars to play in the league.

PORTLAND
TRAIL BLAZERS
SACRAMENTO
KINGS
GOLDEN STATE
WARRIORS
UTAH JAZZ
DENVER
NUGGETS
LOS ANGELES
CLIPPERS
LOS ANGELES
LAKERS
PHOENIX
SUNS
OKLAHOMA CITY
THUNDER
DALLAS
MAVERICKS
SAN ANTONIO
SPURS
HOUSTO
ROCKET

NATIONAL BASKETBALL ASSOCIATION MAP

TIMELINE

1891

James Naismith assembles two teams of nine players each to test out a new recreational activity that he called *basket ball.* The first public game would be held several months later, in early 1892.

1926

The Harlem Globetrotters are established. The traveling team would become famous around the world, delighting fans in more than 120 countries with awesome skills, deft ball handling, and amazing trick shots.

1946

The Basketball Association of America is founded.

1949

The BAA merges with the National Basketball League to form the National Basketball Association.

1954

The shot clock is adopted to limit offensive stalling and increase excitement. Scoring immediately increases, and the game is changed forever.

1957

Bob Cousy and Bill Russell lead the Boston Celtics to their first NBA championship.

1960

The Minneapolis Lakers relocate to Los Angeles, becoming the first NBA team to operate on the West Coast. Two years later, the Philadelphia Warriors would move west to San Francisco.

1967

The American Basketball Association is launched, introducing pro basketball in many cities that would ultimately become NBA strongholds. The ABA would be known for an exciting style of play, popularizing the 3-point shot and dunk contest, and using a red, white, and blue basketball.

1969

The Celtics win their 11th and last championship with Russell. Among their titles was a streak of eight in a row from 1959 to 1966.

1976

Four ABA teams—the Denver Nuggets, Indiana Pacers, New York Nets, and San Antonio Spurs—are absorbed into the NBA as the rival league ceases operations.

1979

Magic Johnson and Larry Bird make their NBA debuts, ushering in a new era of superstardom and popularity for the league.

1984

Michael Jordan is drafted No. 3 overall and makes his NBA debut with the Chicago Bulls.

1992

The US Olympic basketball team features NBA players for the first time. The squad, nicknamed "The Dream Team," dominates the competition and wins a gold medal in Barcelona, Spain.

1997

The Women's National Basketball Association debuts, with MVP Cynthia Cooper leading the Houston Comets to the first league championship.

1998

Jordan leads the Bulls to their sixth NBA championship. It is their second "three-peat" of the decade.

2002

China native Yao Ming is drafted No. 1 overall and makes his NBA debut for the Houston Rockets. His success inspires an explosion of basketball popularity in the world's most populous nation.

2010

The Los Angeles Lakers defeat the Boston Celtics in the NBA Finals, giving Phil Jackson his record 11th league championship as a head coach.

2016

LeBron James leads Cleveland to its first championship. The Cavaliers defeat the Golden State Warriors in seven games, becoming the first team ever to overcome a 3–1 deficit in the best-of-seven NBA Finals.

2018

Kevin Durant and Steph Curry lead the Warriors to their third NBA title in four years, beating the Cavaliers in the Finals each time.

THE WINNERS

BOSTON CELTICS: 17

Bill Russell led the Celtics to 11 championships in 13 seasons from 1957 to 1969. That unprecedented run set the Celtics up for basketball lore, and future generations kept the tradition going. Later groups led by John Havlicek, Larry Bird, and then Paul Pierce also won championships in Boston.

MINNEAPOLIS-LOS ANGELES LAKERS: 16

Many of the Lakers' titles were won on the shoulders of three dominating big men—George Mikan, Kareem Abdul-Jabbar, and Shaquille O'Neal. Legendary shooters Jerry West and Kobe Bryant also contributed. Together, these players have helped create several generations of greatness.

CHICAGO BULLS: 6

The all-around excellence of Michael Jordan and Scottie Pippen, coupled with the coaching acumen of Phil Jackson, made Chicago the center of the basketball universe in the 1990s. The Bulls twice won three championships in a row. Jordan was the MVP of all six NBA Finals.

PHILADELPHIA-GOLDEN STATE WARRIORS: 6

The Philadelphia Warriors won the 1947 BAA championship and added an NBA title in 1956. Upon moving to the West Coast, Rick Barry led Golden State to the 1975 title before Stephen Curry, Klay Thompson, and Draymond Greene took over in the 2010s.

SAN ANTONIO SPURS: 5

Game-changing power forward Tim Duncan relied on a supporting cast that included center David Robinson and athletic guards Tony Parker and Manu Ginobili over the years.

**Accurate through the 2017–18 season.*

THE BIG THREE

A collection of top performers in various statistics.

MOST MVP AWARDS

1. Kareem Abdul-Jabbar: 6
2. Michael Jordan: 5
   Bill Russell: 5

MOST CAREER POINTS

1. Kareem Abdul-Jabbar: 38,387
2. Karl Malone: 36,928
3. Kobe Bryant: 33,643

HIGHEST CAREER POINTS PER GAME

1. Michael Jordan: 30.12
2. Wilt Chamberlain: 30.07
3. Elgin Baylor: 27.36

MOST CAREER REBOUNDS

1. Wilt Chamberlain: 23,924
2. Bill Russell: 21,620
3. Kareem Abdul-Jabbar: 17,440

MOST CAREER ASSISTS

1. John Stockton: 15,806
2. Jason Kidd: 12,091
3. Steve Nash: 10,335

MOST CAREER STEALS

1. John Stockton: 3,265
2. Jason Kidd: 2,684
3. Michael Jordan: 2,514

MOST CAREER POINTS (WNBA)

1. Diana Taurasi: 7,867
2. Tina Thompson: 7,488
3. Tamika Catchings: 7,380

MOST CAREER REBOUNDS (WNBA)

1. Tamika Catchings: 3,316
2. Lisa Leslie: 3,307
3. Rebekkah Brunson: 3,186

**Accurate as of April 2018.*

FOR MORE INFORMATION

BOOKS

Abdul-Jabbar, Kareem. *Becoming Kareem: Growing Up on and off the Court*. New York: Little, Brown Books for Young Readers, 2017.

Bryant, Howard. *Legends: The Best Players, Games, and Teams in Basketball*. New York: Philomel Books, 2017.

Williams, Doug. *Great Moments in Olympic Basketball*. Minneapolis: Abdo Publishing, 2014.

ON THE WEB

Basketball Reference
www.basketball-reference.com

Hoops Hype
www.hoopshype.com

Naismith Memorial Basketball Hall of Fame
www.hoophall.com

NBA
www.nba.com

Remember the ABA
www.remembertheaba.com

WNBA
www.wnba.com

PLACES TO VISIT

MADISON SQUARE GARDEN

4 Pennsylvania Plaza
New York, NY 10001
www.msg.com/madison-square-garden

The enduring center of the basketball universe, MSG is unsurpassed for its classic game atmosphere during New York Knicks or college games.

NAISMITH MEMORIAL BASKETBALL HALL OF FAME

1000 Hall of Fame Avenue
Springfield, MA 01105
www.hoophall.com

Located in the city where the sport itself was created, the Basketball Hall of Fame is a museum dedicated to the game's history, evolution, and greatest figures. You can even shoot hoops on a variety of baskets used through the years, including a peach basket.

SELECT BIBLIOGRAPHY

BOOKS

Editors of Sports Illustrated Magazine. *Sports Illustrated Basketball's Greatest*. New York: Time Home Entertainment Inc., 2014.

Encyclopedia of Ethnicity and Sports in the United States. Westport, CT: Greenwood Press, 2000.

Grasso, John. *Historical Dictionary of Basketball*. Lanham, MD: Scarecrow Press, 2011.

Porter, Karra. *Mad Seasons: The Story of the First Women's Professional Basketball League*. Lincoln: University of Nebraska Press, 2006.

ONLINE

Barreiro, Dan. "The Fab Five: Led by George Mikan, the Minneapolis Lakers–Basketball's First Dynasty–Ruled the League with Five Titles in Six Seasons." *NBA.com*. n.d. http://www.nba.com/encyclopedia/minneapolis_lakers.html. Accessed 1 Mar. 2018.

Bulik, Mark. "1892: A Newborn Called 'Basket Ball.'" *New York Times*. 3 March 2015. https://www.nytimes.com/times-insider/2015/03/03/1892-a-newborn-called-basket-ball. Accessed 1 Mar. 2018.

Fischer-Baum, Reuben. "The Warriors Still Aren't the Best Team Ever." *FiveThirtyEight*. 19 May 2016. https://fivethirtyeight.com/features/the-warriors-still-arent-the-best-team-ever. Accessed 1 Mar. 2018.

Medina, Mark. "Magic Johnson on Larry Bird: 'We're Mirrors of Each Other.'" *Los Angeles Times*. 12 April 2012. http://articles.latimes.com/2012/apr/12/sports/la-sp-ln-la-magic-johnson-on-larry-bird-were-mirrors-of-each-other-20120412. Accessed 1 Mar. 2018.

INDEX

ABOUT THE AUTHOR

Thomas Neumann has been a basketball fan since childhood, when he sat in the upper deck at the old HemisFair Arena to watch the San Antonio Spurs. Neumann is a longtime sportswriter and editor who has worked at ESPN and the *San Diego Union-Tribune.* He lives in Sarasota, Florida, with his wife and two sons.